A Note from Michelle about
THERE'S GOLD IN MY BACKYARD!

Hi! I'm Michelle Tanner. I'm nine years old. You'll never guess what I just found out. My house was built on top of an old gold mine. For real! Now I can buy this cool bike I saw in a magazine. All I have to do is dig up the gold in my backyard to pay for it. And I can't wait to start shopping for lots of awesome presents for my family! Good thing I'm going to be rich because that's a lot of people.

There's my dad and my two sisters, D.J. and Stephanie. But that's not all.

My mom died when I was little. So my uncle Jesse moved in to help Dad take care of us. So did Joey Gladstone. He's my dad's friend from college. It's almost like having three dads. But that's still not all!

First Uncle Jesse got married to Becky Donaldson. Then they had twin boys, Nicky and Alex. The twins are four years old now. And they're so cute.

That's nine people. And our dog, Comet, makes ten. Sure, it gets kind of crazy sometimes. But I wouldn't change it for anything. It's so much fun living in a full house!

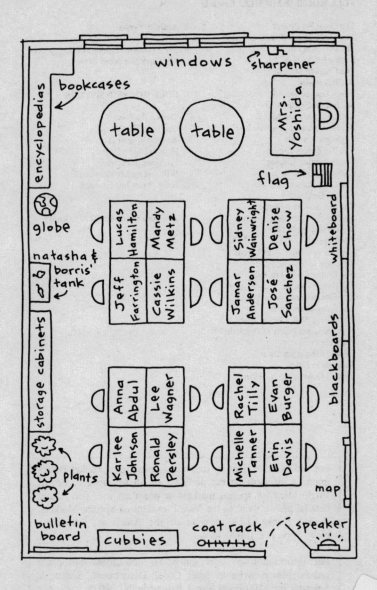

FULL HOUSE™ MICHELLE novels

The Great Pet Project
The Super-Duper Sleepover Party
My Two Best Friends
Lucky, Lucky Day
The Ghost in My Closet
Ballet Surprise
Major League Trouble
My Fourth-Grade Mess
Bunk 3, Teddy and Me
My Best Friend Is a Movie Star!
    (Super Special)
The Big Turkey Escape
The Substitute Teacher
Calling All Planets
I've Got a Secret
How to Be Cool
The Not-So-Great Outdoors
My Ho-Ho-Horrible Christmas
My Almost Perfect Plan
April Fools!
My Life Is a Three-Ring Circus
Welcome to My Zoo
The Problem with Pen Pals
Tap Dance Trouble
The Fastest Turtle in the West
The Baby-sitting Boss
The Wish I Wish I Never Wished
Pigs, Pies, and Plenty of Problems
If I Were President
How to Meet a Superstar
Unlucky in Lunch
There's Gold in My Backyard!

Activity Books

My Awesome Holiday Friendship Book
My Super Sleepover Book

FULL HOUSE™ SISTERS

Two on the Town
One Boss Too Many
And the Winner Is . . .
How to Hide a Horse
Problems in Paradise
Will You Be My Valentine?
Baby-sitters Incorporated

Available from MINSTREL Books

Full House™

Michelle
and Friends

THERE'S GOLD
IN MY BACKYARD!

Judy Katschke

A Parachute Press Book

A MINSTREL®
BOOK

Published by POCKET BOOKS
New York   London   Toronto   Sydney   Singapore

A MINSTREL PAPERBACK *Original*

A Minstrel Book published by
POCKET BOOKS, a division of Simon & Schuster Inc.
1230 Avenue of the Americas, New York, NY 10020

A PARACHUTE PRESS BOOK

 ™ Copyright © and ™ 2000 by Warner Bros.

ISBN: 0-671-04197-5

First Minstrel Books printing May 2000

10   9   8   7   6   5   4   3   2   1

A MINSTREL BOOK and colophon are registered trademarks of
Simon & Schuster Inc.

Clothing in cover art courtesy of Space Kiddets

Printed in the U.S.A.

Chapter 1

♥ "It's perfect!" nine-year-old Michelle Tanner whispered to herself. She stared at the picture of the shiny red bicycle in the magazine. "It's totally perfect!"

Michelle ran into the kitchen. "Dad! Dad!" she cried, waving the magazine.

Danny Tanner looked up from the meat loaf he was forming into a pineapple shape. His wildly colored Hawaiian shirt clashed with the flowered lei around his neck.

"Aloha," he said. "My pineapple luau meat

loaf will be ready in an hour. Grass skirt required."

Michelle's dad was the host of a TV show called *Wake Up, San Francisco*. He also loved to cook. So much that he decided to have a Dinner around the World Week at home. Michelle didn't want to talk about meat loaf, though. She wanted to talk about the Red Hot Roadrunner!

"I found it, Dad!" Michelle cried. "I found it!"

Danny poured some pineapple chunks on the meat loaf. "You found the remote control?"

"No—this." Michelle held up the picture of the bicycle. "Can I have it, Dad? Please?"

"You already have a bike, Michelle," Danny said.

"Not like this one," Michelle declared. "This is the Red Hot Roadrunner. It's got streamers on the handlebars and three speeds. It's the bike of my dreams."

"Your bike is still in great shape, Michelle," Danny replied. "It *rides* like a dream."

"But my bike is a hand-me-down," Michelle complained. "It belonged to D.J., then to Stephanie, and now to me. I'll bet *you* even rode it when you were a kid, Dad."

"You mean in the Stone Age?" Danny joked. He shook his head. "They hadn't invented the wheel yet."

Michelle rolled her eyes. Her dad just didn't get it. "I want something that's all mine for a change," she told him. "Not another hand-me-down." She held up the magazine again and smiled. "Besides, this is the *perfect* bike for a fourth-grade class president like me. Right?"

"Sweetie," Danny began, "apples grow on trees, peaches grow on trees, even pineapples grow on trees—"

"I thought pineapples grew on bushes," Michelle interrupted.

Danny cleared his throat. "Oh. Well, the

3

point is that money doesn't grow on trees, either."

"So if we were rich, I could have it?" Michelle asked.

"Michelle, if we were rich, we'd be living in a much bigger house," Danny said. "We could sure use the space."

Michelle agreed with that. Nine people lived in the Tanner home. There were her sisters, Stephanie and D.J., Michelle, and her dad. Her uncle Jesse lived on the third floor with his wife Becky and their four-year-old twin boys, Nicky and Alex. In the basement apartment was her dad's best friend, Joey Gladstone.

"I guess that means I can't have the Red Hot Roadrunner," Michelle said, staring at the magazine.

"I'm sorry, Michelle," Danny said. "But your bike is still good. You can probably ride it until—"

"Until Nicky and Alex get it," Michelle finished for him. She tucked the magazine under her arm and headed out the kitchen door. Once outside she plopped down on the doorstep. Comet, the family's dog, trotted over and licked her hand.

"I know money doesn't grow on trees, Comet," Michelle said. "But if it did, I'd be the first one with a ladder."

"Hey, Michelle!" a voice called. "What's up?"

Michelle looked up. Her thirteen-year-old sister, Stephanie, placed a backpack on the doorstep and sat down.

"Hi, Steph," Michelle said. She held up the picture of the Red Hot Roadrunner. "Check it out."

Stephanie let out a whistle. "Pretty cool! Did Dad say he'd buy it for you?"

"Not unless he wins the lottery," Michelle answered.

"I hear you," Stephanie said. "Better start saving up now. You get a weekly allowance."

Michelle perked up. Why hadn't she thought of that?

"I get three dollars a week," Michelle said. "How long do you think it would take?"

"Let's do the math." Stephanie pulled a calculator from her backpack. "If you save three dollars a week—"

"Um, a dollar seventy-five," Michelle said quickly.

"Why a dollar seventy-five?" Stephanie asked.

"I need a dollar twenty-five for pizza every Wednesday," Michelle explained. "Extra cheese."

"Okay," Stephanie said. "If you put away a dollar seventy—"

"Wait!" Michelle said. "Each week I give fifty cents to a different charity. This week it's Save the Bull Seals."

Stephanie rolled her eyes. "If you put a dollar twenty-five away each week—"

Michelle grabbed Stephanie's arm. "No—wait! The ice-cream truck rolls around every Saturday. Toasty Bars are up to seventy-five cents now."

"That leaves you with only fifty cents," Stephanie replied.

Michelle shrugged. "Benjamin Franklin once said a penny saved is a penny earned. We learned that in school."

Stephanie punched out the numbers on her calculator. "According to this, by the time you have enough money to buy the bike, you'll be old enough to drive a *car.*"

Michelle's heart sank. "I guess a penny went a lot farther in Ben Franklin's day."

"Sorry, Michelle," Stephanie said. She patted her sister on the back. Then she went into the house.

Michelle stared at the picture of the Red Hot

Roadrunner as she walked to the front of the house. She wanted the bike so badly!

"Hi, Mi-*chelle!*" a voice called.

Still looking down, Michelle frowned. She knew Rachel Tilly's voice anywhere. Rachel was new to San Francisco. Her dad owned a chain of bakeries all over the country. Rachel was very rich and good at everything—except being nice.

"Hi, Rachel," Michelle said. But when she looked up, she gasped. Rachel was riding by on a shiny red bicycle—just like the Red Hot Roadrunner!

Rachel grinned over her shoulder as she rode away. Her super-long ponytail fluttered in the breeze.

"It's not fair!" Michelle muttered. "Rachel gets everything she wants just because her dad is rich."

Michelle was about to go back into the house when she had an idea. If grown-ups could be rich—why couldn't kids be rich, too? she wondered. Kids like me!

"That does it, Comet." Michelle carefully tore the picture of the shiny red bike from the magazine. "I'm going to be rich. Then I'll be able to buy whatever I want!"

Chapter 2

♥ Michelle wrote the words *game show* in her notebook as she sat in class Monday morning. She grinned. Her get-rich-quick list was growing right before her eyes.

"Let's see," Michelle mumbled. She ran her finger down the list. "So far I have to buy a lottery ticket, play the stock market, or find a long-lost and very rich relative."

"Michelle?" Mrs. Yoshida called out.

Michelle's head jerked up as she snapped out of her daydream. "Yes, Mrs. Yoshida?"

"Do you know the answer to the question?" Mrs. Yoshida asked.

"The . . . question?" Michelle gulped.

What question? She was so busy making her get-rich-quick list that she wasn't paying any attention to her lesson.

Rachel raised her hand from the desk next to Michelle's. "I know the answer, Mrs. Yoshida," she announced. "The sixteenth president of the United States was Abraham Lincoln."

Hey! Michelle thought. I knew that.

"Very good, Rachel," Mrs. Yoshida said.

Rachel flashed a triumphant smile at Michelle.

Michelle looked over at her best friends, Cassie Wilkins and Mandy Metz, and shrugged.

"Now." Mrs. Yoshida opened a map of California in the front of the room. "How many of you have heard of the California Gold Rush?"

Erin Davis waved her hand from the seat in front of Michelle's. "Ooh—I did!" she said.

"There was a sale on gold earrings at Marren's Department Store. My mother and her friends *rushed* to buy some."

Mrs. Yoshida smiled. "That was a nice try, Erin. But the earrings weren't the answer I was looking for."

"And they probably weren't *real* gold anyway," Rachel added.

"Were so!" Erin snapped back.

"Girls," Mrs. Yoshida warned. She turned to the map. "In 1849 people from all over the world came to California to dig for gold. They wanted to get rich quick."

Just like me, Michelle thought. The quicker, the better.

"They were called miners or prospectors," Mrs. Yoshida said. "But they didn't always *dig* for gold. Sometimes they used a tin pan to swish for gold in the river."

Sidney Wainwright raised her hand. "Is there still gold here in California?"

"Many of the prospectors left before all the gold was mined," Mrs. Yoshida said. "So there probably is."

Excited whispers filled the classroom.

"Here's where we come in," Mrs. Yoshida said. "Each fourth-grade class has been assigned to do a special project on the Gold Rush. Ms. Barnett's class has already copied an authentic prospectors' map."

Ronald Persley leaned over and whispered to Michelle. "Isn't that Victor Velez's class?" he asked.

Michelle nodded over her shoulder. Victor was the vice president of the fourth grade. Michelle had chosen him herself.

"Their map shows all the sites where gold was believed to be," Mrs. Yoshida went on. "And some sites were right here in our own neighborhood."

"Wow!" someone in the back of the room exclaimed.

"Cool!" Mandy cried.

Denise Chow raised her hand. "What kind of a project are we going to do, Mrs. Yoshida?"

"Why don't you take a look at the map in the hall?" the teacher suggested. "Maybe you'll come up with some ideas of your own."

Mrs. Yoshida spent the rest of the morning reading real letters that miners had written home to their families.

When it was time for lunch, the kids filed out of the classroom and past Ms. Barnett's bulletin board.

"Check it out," Cassie said as they walked over to the prospectors' map.

"It's huge!" Mandy exclaimed. "They probably worked through a whole week of recess to make that map!"

Michelle's eyes opened wide. The map was so big it took up the whole bulletin board. It was decorated with colorful paper and copies of photographs from the 1800s.

"What's that big *X* for?" Cassie asked. She pointed to a big red *X* in the middle of the map.

Michelle moved closer to read the description. "It says there used to be a gold-mining camp on that spot. It was called Gold Rush Sal's."

"There's a picture of the camp," Mandy said. Michelle, Mandy, and Cassie huddled to look at it.

"That's not a camp," Cassie declared. "Where's the volleyball court? And the arts and crafts hut? And the—"

"Cassie, get real," Mandy said. "People didn't go there to roast marshmallows and paint ceramic whales. They went there to dig for gold."

Michelle saw a woman in the picture. She was dressed in a blouse, a long skirt, and was leaning on a pickax.

That must have been Sal, Michelle thought.

With all that gold on her land, I'll bet she was *rich.*

"Wait a minute," Mandy said. "It says that Gold Rush Sal's was shut down before all the gold could be dug up. There was a big earthquake that destroyed most of the camp."

"Do you know what that means?" Cassie squealed. "All that gold might still be buried right here in our own neighborhood."

Mandy grabbed Michelle's arm. "That spot where Gold Rush Sal's was," Mandy said slowly. "Isn't that where your house is now?"

What? Michelle practically pressed her nose against the map. She looked above the *X.* She looked below the *X.* She even looked on each side of the *X.*

"Well?" Mandy asked.

"Is it, Michelle?" Cassie asked excitedly. "Is it?"

Michelle turned to her two best friends. "It sure is!" she gasped.

Chapter 3

♥ "Howdy, partners!" Danny said at the dinner table. He tipped his big white cowboy hat. "Tonight, for Danny's Dinner around the World Week—it's Wild Western Eggs and Grits!"

The Tanners stared at Danny's new dish.

"Yee-ha," Jesse said.

"It looks great, Danny," Aunt Becky said.

Danny turned to Stephanie and smiled. "Well, Steph?" he asked. "What do you think?"

"It's cool, Dad." Stephanie crossed her eyes

as she looked up at her head. "But do we have to wear these goofy cowboy hats?"

Danny looked disappointed. "The hats are from the television studio. I thought they would make you all feel at home . . . on the range!"

He chuckled. No one else did.

"Okay, okay," Danny said. "Take off the hats and dig in."

Michelle was too excited to eat—or even take off her hat. She couldn't wait to tell her family about the gold mine. Before she did that, though, she had to make sure everyone was at the table.

D.J. and Stephanie—check. Dad—present. Uncle Jesse, Aunt Becky, and the twins—here. Uncle Joey . . . Michelle stared at his empty chair.

"Where's Uncle Joey?" Michelle asked.

"Joey had to fly to St. Louis this morning," Danny explained. "He's doing a show at the Chuckle Chamber."

Michelle nodded. Uncle Joey was a stand-up comedian. He told jokes at comedy clubs all over the country.

"So," Danny said, looking around the table. "What's new and different with this family today?"

Michelle opened her mouth to answer, but D.J. beat her to it.

"Guess what?" D.J. said. "The All-College tennis match is in a couple of days. I'm playing in the singles."

"All right!" Danny said. He gave D.J. a thumbs-up. "Go for the gold, D.J."

"Funny you should mention gold, Dad," Michelle said. "Our class just started studying the California Gold Rush."

"That's great, Michelle." Danny held up the breadbasket. "Anyone for hot biscuits?"

"There's more," Michelle said. "Another class made a map of where all the gold mines were supposed to be. One of those mines was right here in our own yard!"

Silence. Everyone stared at Michelle.

"Gold?" D.J. wrinkled her nose. "In *our* yard?"

Michelle's strawberry blond bangs bounced as she nodded. "It was a real mining camp run by a woman named Gold Rush Sal."

Becky shrugged. "It could be possible. There was gold all over California."

"Then what are we waiting for?" Michelle cried. She pumped her fist in the air. "Let's start digging!"

"Whoa, Michelle," Danny said. "Many of the nuggets that people dug up during the Gold Rush turned out to be stuff that only *looked* like gold. It was worthless."

"They even called it fool's gold," Uncle Jesse added.

Michelle sank down in her seat. She thought her family would be just as excited as she was, but they weren't.

"Gold Rush Sal wouldn't waste her time,"

Michelle said. "She looked really serious in the picture."

"Sure." Stephanie chuckled. "Until she became *Fool's* Gold Sal!"

"Gold Rush Sal's camp was one of the most successful mining camps during the Gold Rush," Michelle declared. "But she had to close down after an earthquake."

Uncle Jesse looked surprised. "You're kidding!"

"And Gold Rush Sal was *not* a fool," Michelle went on. "She was a hardworking woman with a dream. A dream of getting rich. So she could buy the things she wanted. Such as a cabin, or a horse, or a—"

"Or a shiny red bike?" Danny asked with a wink.

Michelle lowered her eyes. She felt herself blush.

There was no more talk of gold for the rest of the meal. After Michelle helped clear the table, she put on her cowboy hat and went out into the backyard with Comet.

"Can you imagine a mining camp right here, Comet?" Michelle asked. "I wonder if they did the same things we do in our yard. Like barbecues, birthday parties—"

SNIFF, SNIFF, SNIFF.

Michelle turned to Comet. He was sniffing around an old hole he had dug up the week before.

"What is it, boy?" Michelle asked.

Comet whined as Michelle knelt down and peered into the hole. Inside, she spotted bright, shiny flecks. They looked like flecks of gold!

Michelle ran her hand across the bottom of the hole, then stared at her fingers. They were dusted with the same shiny particles.

It was gold all right!

Michelle jumped up. She took off her cowboy hat and waved it in the air.

"Yee-haaaa!" she shouted. "Our house is sitting on a gold mine!"

Chapter

4

♡ "Are you sure it was gold?" Mandy asked Michelle on the school bus the next morning.

Michelle sat in the seat next to Mandy. Cassie had the seat across the aisle.

"See for yourself," Michelle said, raising a finger. "I still have some flecks underneath my nail."

Cassie and Mandy stared at Michelle's finger. "Oooh!" they exclaimed at the same time.

"With all that gold in your yard, you could be rich, Michelle!" Cassie cried.

"I know," Michelle said. She pulled a note-book from her backpack. "That's why I made this last night."

"What is it?" Mandy asked.

"It's a Living Large Scrapbook," Michelle said, opening the book. "It has pictures of all the things I want to buy—once I become rich, of course."

Cassie leaned over the aisle and Mandy leaned over Michelle's shoulder.

"There's the bike I want," Michelle said, pointing to the first page. "And after that, here's what I'm going to get." She turned the page and her friends gasped.

"A mansion?" Mandy asked. She pointed to a picture of a huge house. "You want to buy a mansion?"

"That's just for Comet," Michelle explained. "Our main house will have eight floors, an Olympic-size swimming pool, and maybe a petting zoo."

"A petting zoo?" Mandy repeated.

"Either that or a water park," Michelle said.

Michelle turned to the next page. It showed a picture of a long white car.

"A limousine?" Cassie's eyes widened.

"It beats taking the school bus," Michelle explained. "But don't worry. There'll be room for all three of us."

"If you want all that neat stuff, Michelle, then you'd better start digging," Cassie suggested. "It might take a long time to find all that gold."

"I know," Michelle said as she closed her scrapbook. "That's why I'm going to start today. Right after school."

"Can we help?" Mandy asked.

"I can bring over my old plastic beach shovels," Cassie volunteered. "After I scrape off the sand."

Michelle smiled. Digging for gold with her two best friends could be fun!

"Okay!" Michelle said. "And when we find the gold—we'll split it and *all* be rich!"

The girls gave each other high fives.

"As class president, maybe I'll even throw in something for the whole fourth grade," Michelle said.

"Like what?" Cassie asked.

"Like a whole sports center right next to the playground," Michelle answered.

"From now on I'm going to call you Gold Rush Michelle," Mandy said with a grin.

Gold Rush Michelle? The words gave Michelle a great idea!

"Hey, Mandy, Cassie," Michelle said slowly. "If Gold Rush Sal could do it . . . why can't I?"

Mandy wrinkled her nose. "Do what?"

"I'm going to start a prospectors' camp right in my own yard," Michelle said. "It'll be for the kids in our class, and I'm going to call it Gold Rush Michelle's!"

"Gold Rush Michelle's!" Mandy repeated. "Cool!"

Michelle couldn't think of anything else the whole day. When she got home after school, she ran straight to the kitchen.

"*Hola!*" Danny said. His huge Mexican sombrero bobbed on his head. He showed her a bowl of tortilla chips. "Today we're having—"

"Mexican food—I know," Michelle interrupted. "Dad, can I have some kids over after school tomorrow?"

"Sure," Danny said. "How many?"

"Um . . ." Michelle tilted her head. "The whole class?"

"The whole class?" Danny cried. "Are you working on some kind of school project?"

"We're digging for gold in the backyard," Michelle said. "But the kids don't know it yet."

27

Danny poured some salsa into another bowl. "What?"

Michelle began counting on her fingers. "I first want to make up flyers and—"

"Back up, Michelle," Danny said. "Digging for gold is a very hard job. Many of the miners in the eighteen hundreds gave up and went home."

Michelle shrugged. "I'm already home."

Danny leaned against the counter and shook his head. "I don't know, Michelle. Your whole class? Digging in our backyard?"

"Please, Dad?" Michelle said. "You're always telling us to go for our dreams. Finding gold is *my* dream!"

Danny pushed the sombrero back on his head and studied her. "Dreams are important," he agreed. He thought for a moment. "Okay, you can do it. As long as you promise not to dig up Aunt Becky's flower beds and to replace any grass sods you dig up."

"All right!" Michelle cheered. "Thanks, Dad!"

"But if anything goes wrong," Danny warned, "your camp will be closed down. Understood?"

"I understand," Michelle told him. "Nothing's going to go wrong. I promise!"

Chapter 5

♥ "Well, what do you think?" Michelle asked Cassie and Mandy the next morning at the coat closet. She showed them a black-and-white flyer. "I made it on my dad's computer. I used the same kind of letters they used in the eighteen hundreds."

"'Dig for Nuggets at Gold Rush Michelle's,'" Mandy read out loud. She nodded. "I like it. I like it."

"I have a whole batch of flyers in my backpack," Michelle said. "I'm going to hand them out to everyone during lunch."

"Are you giving them to everyone in our class?" Cassie asked.

Michelle nodded.

"Even Rachel?" Cassie asked.

"I guess I have to—if I'm giving one to everyone else in the class," Michelle said reluctantly. "Even if she is snooty sometimes."

"*Sometimes?*" Cassie asked.

"Don't worry, she probably won't come," Mandy said. "You know how nothing's good enough for Rachel."

They headed over to their desks.

"Today we're going to talk about the different tools miners used to dig for gold," Mrs. Yoshida said when everyone was seated. She leaned a large cardboard diagram of tools against the blackboard.

We're going to need tools, too, Michelle thought, opening her notebook. I'd better make a list.

31

"Most of the prospectors used shovels to dig for gold," Mrs. Yoshida said.

We have only a few shovels in the garage, Michelle thought. What could we use instead?

Michelle tapped her chin with her pencil.

I know! Alex's and Nicky's plastic beach shovels. Cassie said she'd bring some, too, Michelle thought. We can also dig with spoons. The *big* spoons we use for soup!

Michelle wrote the words *beach shovels* on her list. Right under that she wrote *soup-spoons*.

"Those who searched for gold in the river used metal pans to swish water," Mrs. Yoshida said.

We've got loads of aluminum pie pans, Michelle thought. She added pie pans to her list.

"Another way prospectors found gold was by sifting for it," Mrs. Yoshida said. "They would scoop dirt in a pan filled with tiny holes. The fine dirt would pour through the holes, leaving behind the thicker nuggets."

Michelle stared at her list. What could they use to sift for gold?

"Oh, Mrs. Yoshida?" Rachel called, raising her hand.

"Yes, Rachel?" Mrs. Yoshida asked.

"My father—the famous baker—has dozens of sifters just like that," Rachel said. "He uses them to sift flour."

Who cares? Michelle thought. We're not talking about doughnuts and cream puffs. We're talking about—

"Gold!" Michelle whispered to herself.

The flour sifters could be used to sift for gold, too. They would be great to have at Gold Rush Michelle's!

Michelle looked at Rachel and gritted her teeth.

I don't care if Rachel *is* snooty, Michelle

thought. I've got to get her to come to my prospectors' camp!

"The first dig is today after school," Michelle explained as she handed out her flyers in the lunchroom.

"Wait a minute," José Sanchez said. "What if only one of us finds the gold? Who gets to keep it?"

"Good question," Michelle said. "Since everyone is working as a team, we'll split the gold among all of us."

Michelle watched the kids read the flyers.

"Well?" Michelle asked. "Are you all in?"

Denise nodded. "I'm in. I could use a new computer."

"And I need braces," Lucas Hamilton said.

"Lucas, after all the nuggets we dig up, you can get solid gold braces," Michelle answered with a grin.

"Cool!" Lucas exclaimed.

"I'm in, too," Erin agreed.

"Me, too," Ronald said.

Michelle smiled as every kid at her lunch table raised his or her hand.

But there was still one person she needed to say yes.

Michelle spotted Rachel sitting alone at the next table. She was probably waiting for her friend Sidney to join her. Sidney took longer in the lunch line because she was allergic to practically everything.

Michelle stood up. "Be right back," Michelle told Cassie and Mandy.

She marched over to Rachel without giving herself the chance to change her mind. "Here," Michelle said. She thrust a flyer into Rachel's hands.

"What's this?" Rachel asked.

"I found out that my house was built over a real gold mine," Michelle said. "There was a prospectors' camp there and every-thing."

"So?" Rachel asked coolly.

"So the whole class is coming over to dig for gold," Michelle said. She took a long, deep breath. "I'd really like you to come, too, Rachel."

Rachel took a bite of her sandwich and chewed.

Say yes, Rachel, Michelle thought. You've got to say yes.

"Well, Rachel?" Michelle asked. "Do you want to join my prospectors' camp and—go for the gold?"

Rachel put down her sandwich. She looked up at Michelle.

"You mean dig through mud and worms like some icky little gopher? No way!" Rachel cried. "No *way!*"

Chapter
6

♥ This is a disaster! Michelle thought. No Rachel. No sifters. I've got to make her change her mind.

"Think about it, Rachel," Michelle said. "If we find the gold in my yard—we can all be rich!"

"I'm already rich," Rachel replied.

"You know," Michelle began and leaned casually over the table, "if we find gold, we might get our picture on the covers of all kinds of newspapers and magazines."

Rachel's eyes lit up. "Magazines?" she repeated.

"A bunch of kids finding gold. Magazines love that kind of stuff. We'll be famous!" Michelle told her.

"Yeah," Rachel said slowly. She had a dreamy look on her face. "We'll probably write a best-selling book, and be on that TV show, *Lifestyles of the Lush and Lavish*."

Michelle crossed her fingers behind her back. "So do you think you'll do it?"

Rachel nodded. "Okay. I'll do it."

Michelle pumped her fist in the air. "Yesss!"

Rachel looked at her curiously.

"I mean, yes, that's nice," Michelle said. She placed another flyer on the table. "Give one to Sidney, please."

"Okay, but remember," Rachel said. "If I find one gross bug or worm in your yard, I'm out of there."

"No problem," Michelle answered with a smile.

Now for the *big* question, Michelle thought.

"Rachel?" she asked. "Can you bring some of your father's flour sifters with you?"

"Flour sifters?" Rachel flipped her hair over her shoulder and shrugged. "I guess so."

"Great! Thanks!" Michelle exclaimed.

Her heart was skipping as she returned to her table. "All systems go. We have sifters," Michelle told Cassie and Mandy. "Gold Rush Michelle's is open for business!"

"Pie pans, spoons . . ." Michelle said as she collected tools from the kitchen. She glanced at a plastic pitcher on the counter. "And one pitcher of lemonade."

"You're forgetting something," Danny said as he came into the kitchen.

"What, Dad?" Michelle asked.

Danny opened the oven and smiled. "My special crunchy caramel gold nugget cookies!"

"Cookies!" Michelle cried. "Dad, you're the best!"

"Mmm! Something smells awesome!" D.J. said, running through the kitchen. She grabbed a cookie from the tray.

"Hey!" Michelle complained. "I've got hungry miners to feed!"

D.J. shrugged as she took a bite. "And my big tennis match is today. I need all the energy I can get."

"Teenagers!" Michelle sighed, shaking her head.

Danny helped Michelle arrange the cookies on a plate. Then Michelle placed the pitcher of lemonade and the cookies on the windowsill.

She scooped up an armload of tools and headed out the front door. Comet trotted after her.

Michelle sat on her doorstep to wait for her classmates. She had a terrible thought. What if they didn't come? What if they changed their minds? What if—

"Woof! Woof!" Comet barked.

Michelle glanced up. Cassie and Mandy

were leading the kids up her front walk. Her miners had arrived!

"Welcome to Gold Rush Michelle's!" Michelle called, jumping up.

"Ah-chooo!" Sidney sneezed. "This yard must be full of weeds. I'm allergic to weeds, you know."

Michelle nodded. Sidney really *was* allergic to everything!

"Hey, Michelle. I brought these," José said. He held up a few pairs of dark sunglasses.

"Sunglasses?" Michelle asked. "What for?"

"Because when we dig up all those bright, shiny nuggets," José explained, "we're going to need shades!"

A white truck pulled up in front of the house.

The doors of the truck opened and Rachel stepped out. She was followed by two bakers holding cardboard boxes.

Michelle ran over and peeked into the

boxes. She smiled when she saw shiny silver sifters.

"Thanks a lot, Rachel," Michelle said.

"This means when we find gold, I get to be on the cover of our book," Rachel informed her. "And when we're on TV, let me talk."

Michelle rolled her eyes, but she didn't say anything back to Rachel.

"Follow me to the camp!" Michelle shouted. She led the kids around the house to the backyard. Then she jumped on top of a picnic bench, grabbed a tin pie plate, and banged on it with a soupspoon.

"Attention, prospectors," she said. "Before we start, I just want to go over the rules. They're very important."

The kids gathered around and looked up at Michelle.

"There will be no digging through my aunt Becky's flower beds, and we have to replace the grass sods we dig up," Michelle explained.

All the kids agreed.

"Now!" Michelle said. "Let's dig for gold!"

"Yee-haaaa!" the kids yelled together.

Cassie and Mandy helped Michelle hand out the sifters and the shovels.

"How do we use these things?" Lee Wagner asked. He held up one of the sifters.

"It's easy," Michelle said. "Just scoop up a clump of dirt, then squeeze the handle. The dirt will go through the mesh at the bottom, and any gold nuggets will stay behind in the sifter."

The kids spread out to different parts of the yard. Michelle knelt on the ground between Cassie and Mandy.

She used one of the sifters to scoop up some dirt. She pumped the handle. Nothing happened.

"How come nothing's coming out?" Mandy shook her own sifter.

"This sifter's a piece of junk!" José yelled. He threw his on the ground. "It's full of clumps!"

"So is your head!" Rachel snapped at José. "My father uses only the finest imported cooking tools."

"Yuck!" Denise called out. "This imported cooking tool just dug up a gross worm."

"Hey, you guys!" Lucas called out. "I just found a much better way to sift."

"Really? How?" Michelle asked. She turned around—and gasped.

Lucas was sifting dirt through D.J.'s tennis racket!

"Lucas—NO!" Michelle jumped up.

It was too late. . . .

"Michelle?" D.J. called as she walked into the yard. "I left my tennis racket on one of the lawn chairs, but it's gone. Have you seen it?"

Oh, no! Michelle thought. I'm toast!

Chapter 7

Full House: Michelle and Friends

♥ "Is this it?" Lucas held up D.J.'s tennis racket. It was caked with mud and dirt.

"What did you do to it?" D.J. wailed.

Michelle grabbed the tennis racket from Lucas. "D.J., I am soooo sorry!" she said. "I didn't know Lucas was using your racket to sift dirt."

"*Sift dirt?*" D.J. cried.

Lucas nodded. "Just like the prospectors did when they sifted for gold."

"They used *tennis rackets?*" D.J. demanded. "What did they use to *dig?* Golf clubs?"

45

"Golf clubs—that's an awesome idea!" Jamar Anderson turned to Michelle. "Does your dad have a set?"

"Don't even think about it," Michelle warned him.

D.J. shook her tennis racket. A big chunk of mud fell off. "Oh, great! And I have a big match today."

"Are you going to tell Dad?" Michelle asked slowly.

D.J. crossed her arms. "Don't you think I should?"

"Please don't!" Michelle begged. "If Dad finds out, he'll make me close down my camp!"

"And then we'll never get rich," Mandy called from the patch of dirt she'd been working on.

"Well . . ." D.J. hesitated.

"I'll clean your room for a week!" Michelle promised.

D.J. smiled. "It's a deal. Your secret is safe with me."

"Thanks, D.J.!" Michelle exclaimed as her sister walked back to the house. "And remember—you're helping us make history!"

D.J. looked over her shoulder. *"You'll* be history if you ruin any more of my things."

Lee held up his muddy sifter. "We can't use these, Michelle. What else do you have?"

Michelle ran over to the picnic table and picked up a handful of soupspoons. "We can all use these."

She passed out the spoons, then headed over to her patch of dirt. She knelt down and started to dig.

"It's going to take forever this way!" Jamar complained.

WHIRRRRRR! WHIRRRRR!

Michelle jerked her head toward the sound. "Whoa," she gasped. A small electronic steam shovel was whizzing through the yard. It was bright yellow, with four black wheels and a long red shovel attached to the front.

Comet barked and started to chase it.

"Where did *that* come from?" Michelle cried.

Jeff Farrington poked his head over the bushes. "Yo, Gold Diggers!"

"I've come to help you dig," Jeff said. He held up a remote control. "With my Bigger Digger!"

The little steam shovel came to a halt. Comet sat down and stared at it.

"It's just a toy, Jeff. How is it going to help us?" Michelle asked.

"I'll show you," Jeff said. He walked into the yard and pressed a green button on the remote control in his hand. The steam shovel's shovel lifted slowly. Then it lowered to the ground and began to dig.

"Neato-mosquito!" Ronald declared.

Michelle smiled as the steam shovel

scooped up clumps of dirt and dumped them aside. "Wow! It's a lean, mean, gold-digging machine!" she exclaimed.

"If you think that's cool, watch what happens when I press the supersonic-turbo-switch." Jeff placed a finger on a big black switch. "Three, two, one—blast off!"

Everyone cheered as the steam shovel raced through the yard at top speed. It scooped up dirt as it went.

"Look at it go!" Jeff shouted. He hopped up and down and waved the remote in the air.

Comet sprang to his feet. He leaped at Jeff.

"Ahh!" Jeff shouted and stumbled back. "Your crazy dog wants my remote!"

"Down, Comet," Michelle ordered. "Down, boy!"

It was too late. Comet jumped on Jeff again. The remote control flew out of Jeff's hands— and into the bushes.

"Now look what you made me do!" Jeff told Comet.

"Look!" Ronald Persley shouted. He pointed over Michelle's shoulder.

Michelle spun around and froze. The Bigger Digger was racing toward the back of the yard—and Aunt Becky's flower garden!

Chapter

8

♥ "Oh, no!" Michelle cried. She jumped up and down. "It's digging up Aunt Becky's flowers!"

"Ah-choo!" Sidney sneezed. She rubbed her red nose with a tissue. "I'm allergic to flowers, too!"

"Let's catch it, you guys!" Jamar shouted.

The kids stomped all over the marigolds, gladiolas, and roses as they chased the Bigger Digger.

"Stop!" Michelle yelled. "You're making it worse!"

"My garden!" Aunt Becky's voice cried out.

Michelle whirled around. Danny and Aunt Becky were running out of the house and into the yard.

"Michelle!" Danny demanded. "Stop that truck!"

"I can't, Dad!" Michelle cried. "We lost the remote!"

The truck spun onto its back wheels. It tilted to the side, teetered, then tipped over.

Everyone was quiet as they stared at the ruined garden.

"Bummer," José mumbled.

Michelle couldn't remember when she felt so bad. She had promised her father that they wouldn't dig through the grass or the flower garden. How could she let this happen?

She turned to Aunt Becky. "I'm so, so sorry."

Lee ran over with a big grin on his face.

"Hey, everybody!" he called. "I found the remote!"

The kids stared at Lee as he held up the remote control.

Lee looked at the garden and sighed. "Too late."

"Look at this yard." Danny shook his head as he walked around. He turned to the kids. "It's getting close to dinnertime. Why don't you all pack up and go home?"

Michelle watched the kids collect their things. After they all left the yard, Michelle walked over to her father. He didn't look angry—just very disappointed.

"I was afraid the yard wouldn't survive this project," he said. "Michelle, you and your friends are going to have to find some other way to make your millions."

"We were being really careful. But Comet jumped on Lee and knocked the remote out of his hand and—" Michelle shook her head helplessly. "I promise it won't happen again. I *double* promise."

Her father looked at Aunt Becky. She gave a tiny nod.

"Okay," Danny told Michelle. "You can have one more day."

"Thanks, Dad. Thanks, Aunt Becky," she said. "As soon as we get our gold, I promise I'll buy you tons more flowers."

"Why don't you just set the table, and we'll call it even," Aunt Becky said.

"I'm right on it," Michelle replied.

"Guess what?" D.J. said that evening. She walked into the dining room and held up her racket. "I won the tennis match!"

"Congratulations, D.J.," Danny said. He stared at her tennis racket. "But why is your tennis racket so . . . . dirty?"

Michelle almost spit out her milk. She hoped D.J. would keep her secret.

"Um," D.J. said. "After I won I was so happy that I threw my tennis racket up in the air. And it landed in—"

"A sandbox?" Alex asked, his eyes wide.

"Yeah, that's it," D.J. said, smiling. "A sandbox!"

"I didn't know they had sandboxes in college," Uncle Jesse said. "What's next? Finger painting?"

D.J. glanced at Michelle and smiled. "Uh, probably. I'd better go upstairs and change."

Michelle smiled back. That was close!

"Okay, everyone. In honor of Dinner around the World Week we're having African peanut soup," Aunt Becky announced. She walked over to the table with a big tray of soup bowls.

Soup? Michelle thought in a panic. I didn't know we were having soup!

"It looks yummy," Stephanie said. "I can't wait to taste it, but I don't have a spoon."

"Oh, Michelle," Aunt Becky said. "I forgot

to tell you we were having soup. Could you run into the kitchen and bring in the spoons?"

Michelle gulped. "Um, I kind of used them for my prospectors' camp."

"Oh, no," Uncle Jesse said. "Not our soup-spoons."

"Gross!" Stephanie groaned.

"I'll go get them and wash them all right now!" Michelle cried. She didn't want her dad to change his mind about closing down her prospectors' camp.

"I'll help," Stephanie volunteered. "I'm starving. I need my spoon."

"When we're rich we'll eat in gourmet restaurants every night," Michelle promised everyone. "And none of us will ever have to wash dishes again!"

"So?" Erin whispered to Michelle in class the next morning. "Did your father make you close down your camp?"

"No," Michelle whispered back. "Gold Rush Michelle's is still in business."

"Okay, class," Mrs. Yoshida said. "We learned yesterday that gold is a mineral. But how many of you know that it's also a precious metal?"

Rachel tossed a note on Michelle's desk. Michelle frowned as she opened the paper. Now what did Rachel want?

The note wasn't from Rachel. It was from Jamar! It read:

I HAVE JUST WHAT WE NEED FOR OUR GOLD DIG TODAY!

Michelle leaned over and looked at Jamar. He smiled and gave her a thumbs-up sign.

What could it be? Michelle wondered.

During recess, lunch, and on the school bus, Jamar wouldn't tell Michelle what he had for the gold dig. He said he wanted it to be a surprise. But when they were all in Michelle's backyard, Jamar finally spilled his secret.

"Ta-daaa!" Jamar announced. He held up a long bar with a red light attached to it.

"What's that?" Michelle asked, scrunching her nose.

"It's a metal detection rod," Jamar said. "If gold is a metal, then this thing should find it."

"How does it work?" Mandy asked.

"You just wave it over the ground," Jamar said. "And if it passes over metal, it beeps like crazy. My grandpa found an old Spanish coin on the beach with this thing."

"Wow!" Michelle said. "In that case, go for it!"

Jamar held out the rod. He walked slowly around the yard. Michelle and the other kids followed him.

Then all of a sudden—*BEEP! BEEP! BEEP!*

The kids bumped into one another as they gathered around Jamar and his metal detector.

"What's happening?" Michelle asked.

"It means we found it!" Jamar cried. "We found gold!"

Chapter 9

♥ "Where is it?" Michelle cried. "Where's the gold?"

Jamar pointed to the ground. "It's got to be right under there."

"We have to start digging!" Erin said.

Michelle grabbed a handful of Alex's and Nicky's little beach shovels. "Use these!"

Ronald and Erin snatched two beach shovels from Michelle. They began digging frantically.

"Faster!" Rachel demanded. She took one of the shovels and fanned herself with it. "Dig faster. *Faster.*"

Michelle held her breath as Ronald and Erin dug through the dirt. Jamar's metal detector wouldn't lie. There *had* to be gold under there.

"I think I found something!" Erin said. She threw her shovel aside and pointed to something silver on the ground.

"What is it?" Sidney asked. She picked up the silver object and turned it over in her hand.

"I don't know," Michelle said, staring at the object.

Stephanie walked into the yard. She looked down at Sidney's hand and smiled. "So that's where it was!"

"What?" Michelle asked.

Stephanie pointed inside her mouth. "My retainer. I lost it more than a year ago. Comet must have buried it."

Sidney dropped the retainer. She began to tremble. "Yuck! Gross!" she shouted. "I must be allergic to dog germs, too!"

Mandy grabbed Sidney by the shoulders.

"Calm down!" she ordered. "The dog spit has dried up by now."

Did Gold Rush Sal have these kinds of problems? Michelle wondered. I don't think so!

Stephanie shrugged. She picked up the retainer and walked back into the house.

"What do we do now?" Cassie asked.

"We keep on digging," Michelle said.

"With what?" Rachel demanded.

Anna Abdul stepped forward. "My mom is a doctor, so I brought tongue depressors." She held up a handful of flat wooden sticks.

"Ahhhh!" Lee laughed and stuck out his tongue.

"Thanks, Anna," Michelle said. "Let's get to work!"

"Not so fast," Rachel said, stepping forward. "It's about ninety degrees out here. Where's our lemonade?"

Michelle gave her forehead a light whack. How could she forget about refreshments?

"I'll go into the house and get a fresh pitcher right now," she promised.

While Anna passed out the tongue depressors, Michelle ran into the kitchen. "The kids want lemonade, Aunt Becky."

"I'll help you make it," Aunt Becky offered.

Michelle shook her head. After yesterday's flower disaster, she didn't want Aunt Becky to lift a finger.

"Thanks, but this stuff is a snap to make." Michelle held up a can of lemonade mix.

She poured three scoops of lemonade mix into the plastic pitcher. Then she added four cups of ice water. After mixing it with a wooden spoon she placed it on the windowsill with a pile of paper cups.

"Come and get it!" Michelle shouted from the window.

The kids jumped up and stampeded to the lemonade. Michelle stared as they quickly gulped it down.

Wow, she said to herself. Gold mining is thirsty work.

When the pitcher was empty, Michelle made another. And another. And another. The kids kept drinking it up!

"Aunt Becky," Michelle said, looking through the cupboard. "We're out of lemonade mix. What do I do?"

"What would Gold Rush Sal do?" Becky asked.

Michelle gave it a thought. She snapped her fingers. "She'd squeeze *real* lemons!"

"Hey, Michelle!" José called through the window. He wiped his sweaty forehead with his sleeve. "How about some more lemonade?"

"In a minute!" Michelle called back. She grabbed a handful of lemons. She let Aunt Becky cut them. Then she squeezed one over the pitcher.

"Ow!" Michelle cried as a stream of lemon

juice hit her in the eye. One lemon down, eight more to go.

"And bring out some cookies!" Evan shouted.

"Coming!" Michelle called back.

She squeezed the rest of the lemons as fast as she could, then added water and sugar. She ran to the cupboard and pulled out a bag of chocolate-chip cookies. She ripped open the package and dumped the cookies on a tray.

"Okay, here I am," Michelle announced. She stepped through the back door with the pitcher and tray.

She saw Victor Velez standing behind the bushes. He was looking into the yard.

"Hi, Victor!" Michelle called. "We're digging for gold. Want to grab a cup of lemonade and help?"

Victor's eyes opened wide. He shook his head hard. "No!" he replied. "I've got to take—a map. I mean a *nap*. I mean—I've got to walk my dog!"

Michelle watched as Victor practically ran away.

"That's weird," Cassie said. "Victor doesn't have a dog."

"What's *with* him?" Mandy asked.

"Maybe he doesn't like lemonade." Michelle placed the lemonade and cookies on the picnic table.

"Well, neither do I," Sidney said. She scratched her arm. "Don't you have any cranberry juice? Lemons make me break out in hives."

"I'm sick of lemonade, too," Lucas groaned. "How about some iced tea for a change?"

Cranberry juice? Iced tea? Michelle thought. I bet all the prospectors at Sal's camp only got to drink water. And I bet they didn't complain half as much.

"Didn't *anyone* find gold yet?" she asked.

The kids shook their heads.

Michelle forced herself to smile. She raised a tired fist in the air. "Well, then let's keep digging!"

"What about the iced tea?" Lucas grumbled.

"I'll see what we have." Michelle started to trudge back to the house. Rachel caught up to her and tugged at the back of her shirt.

"What?" Michelle asked. She wasn't in the mood for Rachel's complaining.

"There *is* someone here who found gold," Rachel whispered. "But she's keeping it all for herself."

"Keeping it?" Michelle's eyes opened wide. "Who?"

Rachel grabbed Michelle's shoulders and turned her in the direction of Mandy. "See for yourself."

Michelle looked at Mandy and felt her stomach twist into a knot. Sticking out of her friend's back pocket was something bright— and *gold!*

Chapter

10

♥ "Do you believe me now?" Rachel whispered.

Michelle saw it, but she couldn't believe it.

"Mandy's not a thief," Michelle whispered back. "Let's just go over and ask—"

"Attention everyone!" Rachel yelled out. "Mandy is stealing our gold!"

"Huh?" Mandy exclaimed.

The kids stopped digging and looked up.

"No way! Not Mandy!" Erin said, shaking her head.

"Mandy wouldn't steal," Cassie agreed.

"Oh, yeah?" Rachel demanded. "Well, if you don't believe me, check out her back pocket."

Silence. Everyone stared at Mandy's pocket.

"It's *true,*" Erin gasped.

"We're supposed to *share* the gold, Mandy," José said angrily. "Remember?"

"We all worked so hard!" Denise complained.

Michelle watched as the kids stood up and walked toward Mandy. Sweat poured down their angry faces.

"You guys!" Michelle called. "I'm sure Mandy can explain!"

Mandy looked as confused as Michelle was.

"Give us the gold!" Denise shouted at Mandy.

"Give us the gold!" the kids shouted together. "Give us the gold! Give us the gold!"

Michelle and Cassie ran over to Mandy.

"Give us the gold!" the kids shouted louder.

"Okay, but I already ate most of it." Mandy reached into her back pocket and pulled out a Goody Gold Candy bar.

Rachel's jaw almost hit the floor. "A candy bar?"

Michelle smiled with relief. "See? All you saw was the gold wrapper. I told you Mandy wasn't a—"

"What's going on out here?" Danny's voice interrupted.

Michelle turned around. Her father and Uncle Joey were standing in the yard. Joey had just come back from his trip to St. Louis. He was carrying a suitcase.

"Hi, Dad. Hi, Uncle Joey," Michelle said. "We were just figuring out more ways to dig for gold."

"It sounded like a fight," Danny said. "I'm

afraid this gold fever is bringing out the worst in you kids."

Oh, no, Michelle thought. Is Dad going to shut us down right here, right now?

"Excuse me," Uncle Joey said. "But what's all this about digging for gold?"

"Our house was built on the site of a real prospectors' camp, Uncle Joey," Michelle explained. "And a few days ago I found gold flecks right here in the yard!"

"Gold flecks?" Joey said. He raised an eyebrow. "Where?"

Michelle pointed to the hole in the back of the yard. "Over there," she said.

Joey let out a long whistle. "Oh, boy."

"What, Uncle Joey?" Michelle asked.

"Before I left for St. Louis, I spray-painted a rubber chicken gold out here in the yard," Uncle Joey explained. He forced a smile. "I kind of made a mess."

Michelle gulped. She could practically

feel the kids' eyes on the back of her head.

"A rubber chicken?" Jeff muttered.

"Gold spray-paint?" Denise grumbled.

Rachel stomped in front of Michelle. She planted her hands on her hips. "You mean to tell me we worked so hard for nothing?" she demanded.

"And all we got were a few glasses of sour lemonade?" Lucas asked.

"Sour?" Michelle repeated.

Anna stepped through the crowd. She stared at Michelle with big brown eyes. "I don't get it, Michelle," she said quietly. "When you ran for class president, you said you'd never make a promise you couldn't keep. Now it's like you lied to us."

Lied?

The word hit Michelle like a ton of bricks. She ran for class president to *help* the people in her class, not to let them down.

"But I didn't lie!" Michelle declared.

"Now don't you wish you'd voted for me?" Rachel told the kids. She waved her hand. "Let's go. We're out of here."

Michelle's heart pounded as the kids began walking away. They couldn't leave. Not yet!

Chapter 11

♥ "Wait!" Michelle called from her spot between Cassie and Mandy. "You can't quit now!"

"Why not?" Rachel asked over her shoulder.

"Because of the map!" Michelle exclaimed. "*X* marks the spot—remember?"

Everyone stopped walking.

"The map said that Gold Rush Sal's was right here," Michelle went on. "And the miners never dug up all of the gold. Which means there's got to be gold here somewhere."

Jamar turned to the kids. "Michelle's got a

point. The gold flecks were just paint, but that map *was* for real. Mrs. Yoshida told us so."

"And Michelle didn't know about the paint," Cassie reminded everyone. "It's not fair to say she lied to us."

Michelle raised her arms. "There's still hope, you guys. So we've got to keep on digging."

"And get dirty again?" Rachel replied. She turned to the kids. "We're wasting our time. Come on."

"Go if you want," Michelle said. "But Gold Rush Sal picked this spot. And I trust Sal."

"I'm willing to give it another shot," José said.

"Yeah," Lucas said. He turned toward the others. "Michelle's right. We can trust Sal."

Rachel narrowed her eyes at Michelle. "We'd just better find gold and become famous—or else!"

Michelle smiled at the kids. "Thanks, you guys," she said. "We'll meet here in my yard after school tomorrow."

"Tomorrow?" Danny cried. "I was just about to put an end to this prospectors' camp!"

"Please, Dad!" Michelle begged. "Can't we at least have one more day? Pleeeeease?"

The kids surrounded Danny.

"Please, Mr. Tanner?"

"My mom watches your show every morning!"

"Can we? Can we? Huhhh?"

"Look, Dad. We've been really careful with the yard this time," Michelle added.

Danny ran a hand through his hair. "Okay. One more day," he told them. "But no more fighting. Understood?"

The kids nodded.

Michelle let out a sigh of relief.

What if they didn't find any gold tomorrow?

What if they just found more weeds, worms, and retainers?

I'm not even going to think about that, Michelle decided. Sal didn't quit. And neither will I.

"Now, remember, you guys," Michelle said in class the next morning. "We have only one day left to find the gold, so let's come up with some ideas."

"What if I bring my basset hound, Elmer, to the dig?" Lucas asked. "He can sniff for the gold."

"Good idea," Michelle said. But when she pictured Elmer chasing Comet, she shook her head. "Or maybe not."

"I know," Erin said, hanging up her jacket. "We can have a séance!"

"A what?" José asked.

"That's where people hold hands and talk to spirits," Erin said. "We can ask Gold Rush Sal where the gold is."

"I don't want to talk to ghosts," Rachel snapped.

"And I don't want to hold hands," Lucas grumbled.

Michelle saw Victor walking into their classroom. He looked very worried.

"Hi, Victor," Michelle said. "What's up?"

"I've got to tell you something, Michelle," Victor said in a low voice. "And it's pretty awful."

"What?" Michelle asked. "Did the principal scrap our idea for video games in the lunchroom?"

"Worse." Victor sighed. "It's about our map."

"You mean the prospectors' map?" Michelle asked. "What about it?"

"The X that marked the spot on Gold Rush Sal's," Victor said. He took a deep breath. "It was a joke."

Michelle heard Erin pull in a deep breath.

"A . . . joke?" Michelle gulped.

"Gold Rush Sal's wasn't even near your

block," Victor said. "Two guys in my class stuck that X on the map after it was finished."

"What guys?" Mandy demanded.

"Digger and Doug," Victor said. "They wanted *me* to be class president instead of you," he told Michelle. "The X was their way of getting back at you for winning the election."

"Why didn't you tell me?" Michelle asked softly.

"I wanted to tell you yesterday, but I guess I chickened out," Victor said. "I feel awful, Michelle."

Michelle felt worse. First, the gold specks were just paint. Now the map was just a joke. A big, dumb joke!

"Ah-ha!" Rachel exclaimed. She pointed a finger at Michelle. "I knew it. There was no gold in your yard!"

"We dug all that time in the hot sun!" Denise complained.

"All because Gold Rush Michelle found gold-painted dirt!" Jeff said. "That's even worse than fool's gold!"

Michelle's mouth felt as dry as dust. She began backing up. "I didn't know it was a joke. Nobody told me! I—"

BUMP!

Michelle felt herself crash into someone.

It felt like a grown-up, and there was only one grown-up in her class—Mrs. Yoshida!

"What's this about having the class dig for fool's gold, Michelle?" Mrs. Yoshida asked.

Michelle turned around. Mrs. Yoshida was standing behind her. She looked very serious.

I've got some serious explaining to do, Michelle thought glumly.

Chapter 12

♥ Michelle told Mrs. Yoshida about the map, the gold flecks, even about the Red Hot Roadrunner bike.

"I really wanted to get rich, Mrs. Yoshida," Michelle admitted. "So I made everyone else want to get rich, too."

I'm in for it now, Michelle thought. But when she looked up, Mrs. Yoshida was smiling.

"Boys and girls," Mrs. Yoshida said. "What you experienced was real gold fever. You even got to see what it was like working in a prospectors' camp."

"But we wasted so much time!" Rachel complained. "We could have been working on our class project about the Gold Rush. And it's all Michelle's fault."

Michelle felt her stomach sink.

"It wasn't a waste of time at all," Mrs. Yoshida said. "In fact, all you have to do is write about it, and your Gold Rush project will be complete."

Everyone but Rachel burst into cheers. Cassie and Mandy gave Michelle a big hug.

"Way to go, Michelle," Mandy said.

"That's *Gold Rush* Michelle," Cassie added.

Mrs. Yoshida looked at Victor. "Victor? Shouldn't you be going to your own classroom?"

"Yeah!" Victor said. He turned and ran to the door. "Wait until Digger and Doug hear about this."

"Take your seats, class," Mrs. Yoshida said. "I want to hear all about Gold Rush Michelle's."

81

"Some project," Rachel muttered as they took their seats. "I wanted to make a diorama."

Michelle reached inside her desk to get a pencil. She was glad that something good had come from her gold-mining mess. But she wasn't exactly happy. She saw her Living Large Scrapbook on top of her spelling book and sighed.

Now I'll never be rich, Michelle thought sadly. And I'll never get a new bike. Ever!

Michelle stood in the kitchen and stared at the photo of the Red Hot Roadrunner for a long moment. Then she closed the Living Large Scrapbook and walked over to the recycle bin.

"It was a nice dream," she told Comet. She dropped the scrapbook.

CLUNK!

Comet whined as it hit the bottom of the bin.

"Hey, Michelle," Stephanie said. She walked into the kitchen wearing overalls and rubber gardening gloves. "We're all helping Aunt Becky replant her garden. Want to pitch in?"

"I guess I should help," Michelle answered. "I'm the one who ruined it in the first place."

Michelle and Comet followed Stephanie outside into the yard. Her whole family was kneeling in the back of the yard.

Her dad was digging holes in the ground and D.J. was putting in little plants. The twins then patted around the plants with their plastic shovels.

"Here, Michelle," Uncle Joey said. He smiled and tossed a small shovel at her. "Can you dig it?"

"Sure." Michelle giggled, feeling a tiny bit better. "Where do I start?"

"How about right there?" Aunt Becky said. She pointed to a spot on the ground.

83

"That's exactly where my gladiolas were before."

"Okay, Aunt Becky." Michelle knelt down and began to dig. Suddenly her shovel tapped something hard. She brushed away the earth and spotted something shiny.

Is it gold? Michelle wondered. Her heart started to pound. She brushed away more dirt and found a small gold box.

"What's this?" Michelle asked, picking up the box. She took the lid off and found a note inside. It read:

CHECK OUT THE GARAGE!

Michelle looked at her family. They smiled and shrugged. The twins giggled.

It's a message for *me!* Michelle thought excitedly.

Everyone followed Michelle as she ran to the garage. Danny pressed the remote control. As the door began to rise, Michelle gasped.

Inside the garage was a shiny pink-and-blue bike with silver streamers!

"We fixed up your bike a little," Stephanie said.

"After all," Danny added. "A fourth-grade class president can't ride around on a shabby bike."

Michelle's mouth hung open as she stared at her bicycle. It looked better than new. Even better than the Red Hot Roadrunner!

"Pink and blue are your favorite colors," Nicky said.

"Do you like it, Michelle?" Alex asked.

"It's perfect! It's totally perfect!" Michelle cried. She ran to each member of her family and gave a huge hug. Comet jumped up and licked her face.

"I can't believe you did this for me!" Michelle exclaimed. "Not after I ruined the backyard and used all of our soupspoons for digging, and—"

"And we love you, anyway," her father interrupted her.

Michelle looked at her family. They were all smiling and nodding.

I may not have found gold, she thought. But I *am* the richest girl in the world.

It doesn't matter if you live around the corner...
or around the world...
If you are a fan of Mary-Kate and Ashley Olsen,
you should be a member of

MARY-KATE + ASHLEY'S FUN CLUB™

Here's what you get:
Our Funzine™
An autographed color photo
Two black & white individual photos
A full size color poster
An official **Fun Club**™ membership card
A **Fun Club**™ school folder
Two special **Fun Club**™ surprises
A holiday card
Fun Club™ collectibles catalog
Plus a **Fun Club**™ box to keep everything in

To join Mary-Kate + Ashley's Fun Club™, fill out the form
below and send it along with

U.S. Residents – $17.00
Canadian Residents – $22 U.S. Funds
International Residents – $27 U.S. Funds

**MARY-KATE + ASHLEY'S FUN CLUB™
859 HOLLYWOOD WAY, SUITE 275
BURBANK, CA 91505**

NAME: _MADISon Pinto_

ADDRESS: _2045_

CITY: _William_ ~~BRG~~ STATE: _VA_ ZIP: _____

~~Burge~~ _=590_

PHONE:(___) _____ BIRTHDATE: _APRIl 12_

_46_

1242

FULL HOUSE™
Michelle

A MINSTREL® BOOK
Published by Pocket Books

1033-31

Don't miss out on any of
Stephaine and Michelle's
exciting adventures!

FULL HOUSE™
SISTERS

When sisters get together...
expect the unexpected!

A MINSTREL® BOOK

Published by Pocket Books

2012-03